Dear mouse friends,
Welcome to the world of

Geronimo Stilton

Geronimo Stilton
A learned and brainy
mouse; editor of
The Rodent's Gazette

Thea Stilton
Geronimo's sister and
special correspondent at
The Rodent's Gazette

Trap Stilton
An awful joker;
Geronimo's cousin and
owner of the store
Cheap Junk for Less

Benjamin Stilton
A sweet and loving
nine-year-old mouse;
Geronimo's favorite
nephew

Geronimo Stilton

MERRY CHRISTMAS, GERONIMO!

Scholastic Inc.

New York   Toronto   London   Auckland   Sydney
Mexico City   New Delhi   Hong Kong   Buenos Aires

ISBN 978-0-439-55974-4

Based on an original idea by Elisabetta Dami.

www.geronimostilton.com

Published by Scholastic Inc., 557 Broadway, New York, NY 10012. SCHOLASTIC and associated logos are trademarks and/or registered trademarks of Scholastic Inc.

Stilton is the name of a famous English cheese. It is a registered trademark of the Stilton Cheese Makers' Association. For more information, go to www.stiltoncheese.com

Text by Geronimo Stilton
Original title *É Natale, Stilton!*
Cover by Matt Wolf; revised by Larry Keys
Illustrations by Larry Keys and Blasco Tabasco
Graphics by Merenguita Gingermouse

Special thanks to Kathryn Cristaldi
Interior design by Kay Petronio

40 39 38 37 36 35   16/0

Printed in the U.S.A.   40
First printing, October 2004

LIKE SLIVERS OF GRATED CHEESE . . .

It was the day before *Christmas*.

My alarm clock went off that morning with a loud squeak! I groaned. I hate getting up in the morning. Especially when it's so cold outside. I stared out my window, and that's when I saw them. Snowflakes! Tiny, fluffy white snowflakes. Just like slivers of grated cheese.

I clapped my paws happily. I just love **snow**.

I raced to the telephone to call Benjamin. He's my favorite nephew.

"I have to spend the morning at the office," I told Benjamin. "But we should go to the park in the afternoon. We can build a SNOWMOUSE."

I told Benjamin to wear lots of warm clothes. It was cold outside. Of course, I dressed warmly, too.

Here is what I put on:

1. A thermal undershirt + thermal long johns

2. Two turtlenecks + three heavy cat-fur sweaters

3. A pair of ski pants

4. A down-filled parka with extra padding

5. A long yellow wool scarf

6. A pair of fleece earmuffs + a matching hat

7. A pair of waterproof fur-lined gloves

8. Ten pairs of extra-long socks + a pair of snow boots

I guess you can tell I don't like to be cold. But now I was feeling nice and warm. In fact, I might have been feeling a little *too* warm. I was as hot as an oven at the Greasy Rat Café! Still, I thought about wearing **ski goggles** just in case. But I had put on so many layers, it took ten minutes to try them on!

I thought about wearing ski goggles just in case.

It took ten minutes to try them on!

A FIRST-RAT CHRISTMAS!

Before I left my mouse hole, I looked around carefully. I had been decorating all week. That's because I was having *Christmas Eve dinner* at my place. It was a tradition. Every year, I invited all of my relatives, my friends, my neighbors, my mailmouse, the mouse who cuts my fur, and lots of other rodents to my house. Yes, I guess you could say almost half the town spent *Christmas Eve* with yours truly.

It's a lot of work getting ready for a party. Especially because I am a very particular mouse. I like everything to be absolutely *perfect*.

I had bought a new WELCOME RAT MAT for the entrance. It showed a picture of Santa Mouse on his sleigh. On my front door, I had hung a **wreath** with a yellow bow. And I had made a banner that hung above my living room door. It said:

Merry Christmas, dear mouse friends!

Green garlands with holly berries spruced up my living room. And, of course, I had a Christmas tree. This year, I had found the most beautiful fir tree. It was the perfect shape. It was the perfect size. And it still had its roots! That's right. When Christmas *was over*, I could plant it in my garden. But right now, it was decorated with plastic cheese slices.

I love plants. I guess that's because I have a green paw. I can grow anything. I can

This year, I had found the most beautiful fir tree.

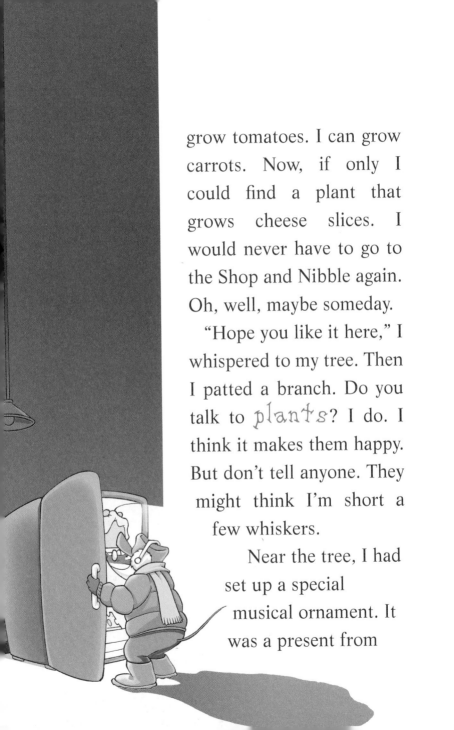

grow tomatoes. I can grow carrots. Now, if only I could find a plant that grows cheese slices. I would never have to go to the Shop and Nibble again. Oh, well, maybe someday.

"Hope you like it here," I whispered to my tree. Then I patted a branch. Do you talk to plants? I do. I think it makes them happy. But don't tell anyone. They might think I'm short a few whiskers.

Near the tree, I had set up a special musical ornament. It was a present from

my great-grandma Tanglefur. It had five golden angels and a red candle in the middle. It played "Frosty the Snowmouse" when I wound it up. Now I lit the candle to see how it looked. I grinned. It was just perfect!

Next, I opened the fridge. On a golden plate sat a cheese-filled gingerbread house. It was covered in icing and decorated with little plastic mice. Some were skiing. Some were building snowmice. It was a real masterpiece. I had bought it from Sugarfurs, the best gourmet sweet shop in New Mouse City. The candy and cookies were super expensive. But they were worth it. Plus, I like to treat myself on Christmas.

I read the evening's menu to myself:

Fresh cheese platter

*

Crêpes with melted cheddar

*

Swiss cheese soufflée

*

Mozzarella mashed potatoes

*

Parmesan pie

*

Gourmet Cheesy Chews

Finally, I checked out my bedroom. My closet was BURSTING with gifts. Boxes of all shapes and sizes filled the shelves. At the bottom of the pile lay three very special gifts.

One of them was for my sister, Thea. (She is the special correspondent at *The Rodent's Gazette*.) It was the latest high-tech compact camera.

For my nephew Benjamin I had

bought a yellow snowsuit. He could wear it skiing. He would look just like **a piece of Swiss cheese** sliding down the mountain.

For my cousin Trap I had bought a cookbook. It was written by one of New Mouse City's most famous chefs, **Saucy Le Paws**. It was called

FROM MY PAWS TO YOURS: RECIPES TO SQUEAK ABOUT!

Saucy Le Paws

I chuckled. No doubt about it. This was going to be a *first-rat Christmas!*

MY NAME IS STILTON . . .

At last, I was ready to head off to the office. Oops! I just remembered. I forgot to introduce myself. I guess I've got too much *Christmas* on the brain. Anyway, my name is Stilton, *Geronimo Stilton*. I'm a **publisher** and a writer. I run a newspaper called *The Rodent's Gazette*. It is the most popular paper on Mouse Island. But maybe you already know me. I don't want to boast, but here in *New Mouse City* I'm fairly well known. Lots of mice have read my funny tales of adventure.

Let's see, where was I? Oh, yes, I was on my way to the office.

Even though I was dressed warmly, I was

still cold. I had mouse bumps everywhere. I wrapped my scarf around my whiskers to keep them from freezing. Still, I wasn't going to let the weather get me down. I love the holiday season. I smiled under my scarf. New Mouse City looked so beautiful under a blanket of snow. The tall buildings sparkled with shiny icicles. And the roads were covered with a fluffy white powder. Rodents of every size, shape, and color rushed here and there. Many carried packages — gifts for their loved ones. I spotted a rodent dressed as Santa Mouse in front of a department store. He was ringing a golden bell. *Ding ding!* "*Merry Christmas to all!*" he squeaked to the rodents passing by.

Rodents of every size, shape, and color rushed here and there.

On one street corner stood a group of young mice. They were singing Christmas carols. I wanted to join in, but I didn't. My sister, Thea, tells me I have a terrible singing voice. I think I sound great. But just in case, I kept my mouth shut. I didn't want to spoil the moment.

Next, I passed by one of New Mouse City's best gourmet cheese shops, Better Cheddar and Beyond. I sniffed the air. It smelled heavenly. I peeked inside. Beautifully arranged were all of those yummy cheeses — warm orange American, holey Swiss, milky white mozzarella.

"You do not need any of those cheeses. Remember, you're on a diet," a little voice inside my head squeaked. I nodded. But before I could leave, I heard another little voice. "It's Christmas, Geronimo," this one said. "Go ahead and treat *yourself!*"

Two seconds later, I was inside the store, **drooling** over two giant **GIFT-WRAPPED BASKETS** of cheese. "I'll take them both," I told the shopkeeper. "Please deliver them to 8 Mouseford Lane." I left before any of the voices could return to yell at me.

As I walked past the toy shop, I noticed an

enormouse stuffed cat in the window. Benjamin would love it, I thought. I decided it would be OK to buy another present for him. After all, he is my favorite nephew. The cat was so big, I had it delivered to my mouse hole. Now I'd have two fabumouse surprises coming in the mail — the cheese and Benjamin's present. Yes, this was going to be one extra-special Christmas!

OFF TO THE NORTH POLE, GERONIMOUSE?

At last, I reached my office at *The Rodent's Gazette.* *"Good morning, everyone!"* I said as I came through the door.

My secretary, Mousella MacMouser, rushed up to me. "Mr. Stilton, I didn't know you were coming in today," she squeaked. "I thought you'd be getting ready for your *Christmas Eve* party."

I smiled. "I've just come in to sign a few papers," I said.

Mousella straightened her glasses. I noticed she was staring at me strangely. "Um, don't take this the wrong way," she mumbled.

"But aren't you hot in that outfit?"

Before I could answer, the door flew open. In raced Benjamin. He was followed by Thea and my cousin Trap.

As soon as Thea saw me, 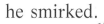 She bURST OUT LaughING. "Gerrykins!" she shrieked, pointing to my getup. "Who dressed you this morning? You look like a giant puffy cheese ball!" Then she collapsed in a fit of giggles.

Trap stuck his snout right up to mine. "Off to the **NORTH POLE**, Geronimouse?" he smirked.

"When are you leaving?"

I rolled my eyes. "First of all, I'm not going to the

North Pole," I squeaked. "And second, my name is Geronimo!"

That made my cousin roar with laughter. Soon, he and Thea were both rolling around on the floor in hysterics. I sighed. Those two are as different as a carton of cottage cheese and a box of caramel Swiss Cheesy Chews. But they have one thing in common. They love to tease me.

Only Benjamin didn't crack up. Instead, he gave me a hug. My parka was so puffy, he sunk right in. "We just came by to say hi, Uncle Geronimo," he explained. Then he leaned close and whispered in my ear. "Good thing you dressed up warmly," he said. "It's colder than the freezer at The Icy Rat. Perfect for building a SNOW MOUSE!"

Benjamin gave me a hug.

MERRY CHRISTMAS, GERONIMO!

I turned my back on Thea and Trap. *Go ahead, laugh all you want*, I thought. *At least my tail won't freeze off in the snow.*

Then I patted Benjamin's paw. "I just have to do a few things here," I told my nephew. "But later, we can PLAY and build ten snow mice, if you like."

When they had left, I headed down the hall toward my office.

I passed through the art department. TYLERAT TRUEMOUSE waved a paw at me. Tylerat is my senior designer. "Merry Christmas, Mr. Stilton!" he squeaked. Then he added with a chuckle, "Aren't you *HOT*?"

I shook my head no and stumbled right

into Tylerat's assistant. "Merry Christmas, Mr. Stilton!" squeaked Merenguita Gingermouse. I could tell she was trying not to laugh. "Aren't you *HOT*?" she finally managed to gasp.

I shook my head no again.

Then it was Cheesita de la Pampa's turn. Cheesita has a head of dark shiny curls. She is usually a shy mouse, but not this morning. "Mr. Stilton, you must be sweating your fur off in that outfit!" she blurted out. "Aren't you *HOT*?" Then she covered her mouth. I could hear her giggling behind her paw. She raced off before I could answer.

Just then, *Sweetie Cheesetriangle* came barreling up to me. Sweetie is my editor in chief. I guess you

TYLERAT TRUEMOUSE

could say Sweetie is the opposite of Cheesita. Sweetie loves to squeak her mind.

"Geronimo! Why are you dressed like that?" she guffawed. "Aren't you *HOT*? At least unzip your parka!"

By now, I was getting annoyed. Why couldn't everyone just mind their own business? "I'm fine! I'm ab-so-lute-ly, pos-i-tive-ly fine!" I shrieked. I whirled around and slammed right into **RODNEY**

Merenguita Gingermouse

Cheesita de la Pampa

RODNEY RATFINKLE

RATFINKLE. Rodney works on our website. He gawked at me from behind his glasses.

"Stilton, you must be *HOTTER* than a burrito at the Spicy Mouse Smoke House!" he screeched, laughing. He reached out to pat my parka.

I shrugged him off. "I'm not hot!" I squeaked. I was fuming. What was with everyone today? So what if I had a few extra layers on. It was cold outside. I mean, OK,

Sweetie Cheesetriangle

Larry Keys, Blasco Tabasco, and Matt Wolf

maybe I'd overdone it with the furry sweaters. And the ski pants were a bit much. But it was my choice to wear them.

I was still furious when I stumbled into a group of **ILLUSTRATORS**. **Larry Keys, Blasco Tabasco,** and **Matt Wolf** gave me the once-over. *Here it comes,* I grumbled to myself.

"Hi, there, Geronimo!" they all squeaked in unison. Three pairs of eyes swept over me. They hooted with laughter. "Aren't you —?"

"No!" I answered before they could finish. They looked shocked. But I didn't care. I'd had it. Why couldn't everyone just leave me alone?! So I had overdressed. So I looked like a giant puffy cheese ball. So what?! I stormed off.

"He needs a vacation," I heard someone whisper. "Looks like he's ready to SNAP!" said another.

I marched through the press room. The press was churning out the latest copy of the newspaper. The noise was deafening. *At least no one could tease me here,* I thought. It was so noisy, I could hardly hear myself think.

Two seconds later, **Pinky Pick** rushed up to me. Pinky is my assistant editor. There is only one word to describe Pinky. LOUD. Yes, Pinky is only a tiny mouse, but she is the loudest mouse I know.

"Hi, Boss —" she called out. I cut her off before she could

Pinky Pick

continue. I knew what was coming next.

"No!" I shouted,

Nooooooooo!

"I'm not, I'm not, I'm not!!!"

She stared at me, puzzled. "What's the matter, Boss?" she squeaked. "I was just going to say *Merry Christmas.*"

I gulped. I felt awful. I didn't mean to yell at Pinky. I was just so tired of everyone teasing me. I was sure Pinky was next. "Er, yes, well, same to you, Pinky," I mumbled.

I **RACED** for my office. Maybe I did need a vacation. Now I was picking on poor little Pinky. And on Christmas Eve, too. I felt awful. I felt ashamed. I felt someone tugging on my paw. I looked down. It was

Pinky Pick. She must have been following me.

"Hey, Boss!" she smirked. "What's with the CRAZY costume? Aren't you HOT under there?"

I groaned. I flung myself into my office. Then I LOCKED the door behind me. Alone at last! I quickly changed into one of the spare suits I keep in my closet. Pheeew!

Yes, I must admit I was hot in my outfit. In fact, I had reached the **boiling point**. I was sweating like a plus-size mouse in the Rattytrap Jungle!

I poured myself an ice-cold cheese coffee. Then I sat down at my desk. *Think COOL thoughts,* I told myself. It took ten minutes for my fur to stop sweating.

THOUSANDS OF SMALL GOLD BALLS

A few minutes later, I heard **TIRES SQUEALING** outside my window. If you ask me, New Mouse City drivers are the worst. They love to go fast. And they love to slam on the brakes. It's crazy. Plus, all of that stopping and starting can be really

tough on a mouse. Whenever I take a taxi, I have to see a chiratpractor the next day.

I rubbed my neck. Just thinking about those taxi rides could make my neck hurt. Suddenly, a **strange** sound interrupted my thoughts.

I twirled my whiskers. What was that noise? It sounded like something bouncing. **Boing! Boing! Boing!** Yes, it sounded like something bouncing along the road.

Ratbury

Curious, I ran outside. I was met by an unbelievable sight. The street was covered with thousands of small gold balls!

A huge delivery truck sat in the middle of the road. It was blocking traffic. A crowd of rodents stood by, talking about the ACCIDENT. They said the driver had SKIDDED on the ICE. It seemed he had swerved to avoid hitting a young mouse who was RUNNING across the street. The truck had been carrying ten thousand *Ratbury* Ratballs.

I picked up one of the gold balls. It had the familiar *Ratbury* logo on it. Each candy was wrapped in glittering gold foil. Have you ever tried

Ratbury

Ratbury Ratballs? They are whisker-licking good.

Right then, I heard someone **SOBBING**. A rat sat on the sidewalk with his head in his paws. I read the back of his shirt. RATBURY, it said. I guessed it was the driver of the truck.

RATBURY RATBALLS!

I went up to him. "Anything I can do to help?" I asked.

The driver stared up at me. "I'm a dead rat," he SOBBED. "I was supposed to deliver ten thousand *Ratbury* Ratballs to the mayor's mansion for the big Christmas banquet tonight. But I had to ▓▓▓▓ ▓▓ ▓▓▓▓ to avoid an accident, and now the Ratballs are all over the road. I'll be fired for sure!"

Tears rolled down his fur. He hung his head in despair. "What a sad, sad Christmas," he bawled. "I have five ratlings to feed at home. I need this job to pay the bills."

I sat down by his side. *Just thinking*

about those poor hungry ratlings made me want to cry, too.

I stared down at the *Ratbury* Ratball in my paw. It was splashed with **mud** and **snow**. Carefully, I wiped it clean with the sleeve of my jacket. The golden foil **shone** just like new. That gave me a great idea!

ANY VOLUNTEERS?

I started counting the rodents in the crowd. Ten, twenty, thirty. Yes, there were at least thirty mice. Plus, the staff of *The Rodent's Gazette* . . .

I jumped to my paws. It would be **MORE THAN ENOUGH!**

I turned my attention to the crowd. "Who will lend a paw here?" I asked. "This **poor** rodent is in an awful jam. If we can **clean up** these chocolates, he can make his delivery to the mayor's mansion."

I waited. No one moved a tail. *Maybe they needed me to show them how,* I thought. I began cleaning off one of the muddy **Ratballs**. When I was done, I placed it in the truck. I grinned at the crowd.

"So, who wants to volunteer?" I squeaked.

Still no one lifted a paw. "I'm too busy," said a mouse, staring at her watch.

"Not today. I have presents to buy," chimed in another, rushing away.

I couldn't believe it. Where was the Christmas spirit? Where was the feeling of goodwill? Where was my nice warm parka? I had left it back in the office. I was freezing my whiskers off!

Just when I thought I would die from the cold, an **elderly** mouse spoke up.

"I will help," he croaked in a feeble voice. "Christmas is not all about presents, you know."

Then he bent over, leaning on his cane. He picked up a *Ratbury* Ratball. He polished it with his PAWKERCHIEF.

Now there were two shiny Ratballs back in the truck. Two down, nine thousand nine hundred and ninety-eight to go. Hmmm. This was going to take a little bit longer than I thought.

"ANY MORE VOLUNTEERS?" I tried again.

The crowd looked at one another.

After a moment, a biker mouse dressed all in leather picked up a *Ratbury* Ratball.

A mother holding her young mouse by the paw pitched in. "Come on, Pawsley, you can pick up some chocolates, too," I heard her murmur. "Let's help that poor rat!"

Next, a **polished-looking** business rodent set down his briefcase. Soon, he, too, was picking up chocolates. A mailmouse dropped his BAGFUL of letters. The newspaper mouse on the corner left his stand. A group of schoolmice joined in as their teacher watched. Even the rodents at the *Squeak & Brew* left their coffee and cheese Danish to help out.

I ran to my office. I had to round up the staff. "Stop the reading! Stop the writing! **STOP THE PRESS!**" I shouted. "Come give me a paw. We must polish each *Ratbury* chocolate until it shines like **new!**"

By now, many curious rodents had stopped by to see what was going on. Once we explained, they began to help. Soon, there were **more than a hundred** rodents picking up chocolates in front of *The Rodent's Gazette.*

WMICE, a local radio station, sent out the word.

Attention, everyone! Lend us your paws. Come to 17 Swiss Cheese Center and help out a poor rat down on his luck.

The crowd of mice grew and grew. As they worked, they chatted with one another. I listened to everyone **laughing** and joking. It was like a regular party! Now all we needed was a little music. I began to sing one of my favorite Christmas songs, "Santa Mouse Is Coming to Town." Soon, the whole crowd was singing along.

Don't you just love the holiday season? It puts everyone in **such a good** mood. Especially me. I didn't even feel **COLD** anymore.

I watched Benjamin shining chocolates with **PAWSLEY**. I watched my secretary, Mousella, working side by side with the mailmouse.

Before I knew it, I was holding the last *Ratbury* Ratball in my paws. I cleaned it up and gave it to the driver.

"Here you are!" I said cheerfully. "This is

the **very last one of them!**" I told him.

The driver shook my paw. His smile stretched from ear to ear.

"Thank you, Mr. Stillman," he gushed. I could see tears GLITTERING in his eyes.

"Um, yes, well, my name is Stilton," I corrected him. "Geronimo Stilton."

But I don't think he understood. He turned to the crowd. "I want to thank Mr. Stillman and every one of you. *Merry Christmas* to you all!"

"*Merry Christmas!*" the crowd answered.

The driver got into his truck. He waved his 🐾🐾🐾. Then he drove off.

A Triple-spin
Somersault

I was feeling tired but *happy*. I decided to write an article for my paper. I would write about the true meaning of Christmas. It's not about spending lots of money on PRESENTS. It's about being kind to others.

Yes, that is what mice mean when they squeak about the Christmas spirit!

I headed **up THE STAIRS** to my office.

But that's when it happened.

I stepped on something **slippery** . . .

flew up into the air . . .

did a triple-spin somersault . . .

landed right on my snout . . .

tumbled down thirteen steps . . .

and smashed onto the pavement!!!

What had I **slipped on?** I could barely move, but I had to find out. With a groan, I looked up. There it was. It was round. It was dirty. I stretched out my paw and grabbed it. It was a *Ratbury* Ratball.

"Cheese niblets. It wasn't the last one . . . it wasn't the last one," was all I could mutter. Then I fainted.

I woke up with a start. Someone was waving a *smelly jar of grated Parmesan cheese* under my nose.

Minutes later, the ambulance arrived. I was carried away on a stretcher. The sirens wailed as we headed for the nearest HOSPITAL.

Rancid rat hairs! *What a horrible Christmas Eve!*

I'm Too Fond of My Tail!

I came back from the hospital with my paw in a C̱A̱S̱Ṯ. I plopped down at my desk. *OK, enough excitement for one day,* I told myself. Just then, I glanced out the window. I noticed a little old mouse down on the sidewalk. She was about to cross the **STREET** right into the traffic! My fur stood on end. Cars and trucks raced by at *breakneck speed*. She would be squashed for sure!

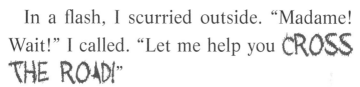
In a flash, I scurried outside. "Madame! Wait!" I called. "Let me help you CROSS THE ROAD!"

She had already taken one step off the pavement. I stopped her in the nick of time.

I gave her my paw (the one without the cast, of course) and helped her to the other side of the road.

"Thank you, young mouse! Merry Christmas!" she MURMURED.

"Merry Christmas to you, too, madame," I answered.

I started walking back to the office. Then

I turned around to wave good-bye . . . and gasped. To my **HORROR**, she was crossing the street again!

Once more, I threw myself back into the traffic. Taxis **whizzed** by me. A bus almost clipped my whiskers. A giant delivery truck **blew** smoke up my snout.

I reached her just in time. "You should have told me you wanted to cross again," I said.

I held up my paw to stop the traffic. Then I helped her to the side of the road again.

"Thank you, young mouse! Merry Christmas!" she MURMURED once more.

With a sigh of relief, I headed toward my office. But I stopped when I heard tires *SCREECHING*.

A tractor trailer had **SLAMMED** on his brakes. Do you know why? That crazy old mouse was crossing the street **again!**

By now, I knew the routine. I threw myself back into the traffic. I saved her by the skin of her dentures.

What did I get for my trouble? A medal? A ten-pound box of Cheesy Chews? A free massage at The Restful Rodent? No. My only reward was a broken tail covered with ▓▓▓▓▓▓▓▓. I stared at it in disbelief. Pain shot through my whole body.

"Putrid cheese puffs!" I shrieked.

The old mouse didn't seem to notice my pain. "Thank you, young mouse! And Merry Christmas!" she MURMURED.

My eyes rolled back in my head. I was about to faint. The last thing I saw was the old lady crossing the street again.

What a dreadful Christmas Eve!

YOU AGAIN?

The **ambulance** arrived. I was put on a stretcher. One of the nurses recognized me. "You again?" he exclaimed.

The other nurse looked down at me. "Ah, it's you again. *Gerald* Stilton, isn't it?"

I wanted to tell him that my name was Geronimo. *Geronimo* Stilton.

But I didn't get the chance. He turned around and tripped over the stretcher. I slid off and landed right on my face. Now I had a bruised snout *and* a broken tail.

They drove me to the HOSPITAL. The

sirens blasted my eardrums. I squeaked in pain. But I couldn't hear my own cry. I couldn't hear a thing. I closed my eyes.

When I came to, I was in a hospital bed. Dr. Mender Mouse was leaning over me. He was WRAPPING up my tail in a cast. "Here again?" he said. "You should be more careful. Why don't you look before crossing the street? Ah, you brainy mice, always with your heads in the CLOUDS. You're a publisher, aren't you, Mr. *Gerolamo*?"

I wanted to tell him about the little old mouse. I wanted to tell him about the truck. I wanted to tell him that my name was not Gerolamo. But I couldn't. He was wrapping up my snout in a cast. I looked just like a MUMMY. All I could do was mumble "Mmmmmmh!"

I WANT TO BE JUST LIKE YOU, UNCLE GERONIMO!

By the time I got back to the office, it was four o'clock. I slumped into my chair. I promised myself I wouldn't stay long. I was drained. I needed to go home.

What a terrible Christmas Eve!

I sighed and told **Mousella** I was leaving.

At least I had everything ready for my dinner party. I thought about the decorations in my living room. I thought about my beautiful fir tree trimmed with cheese ornaments. I thought about the yummy food in my refrigerator. I thought about all of the **presents** I had wrapped for my friends.

I was exhausted.

Benjamin met me in the lobby. "Uncle Geronimo!" he squeaked, worried. "I heard you had an **ACCIDENT**. Are you OK?"

I smiled. It wasn't easy. Have you ever tried to smile when your whiskers are WRAPPED IN PLASTER?

"My dear nephew, I'm fine," I told Benjamin. "No need to worry."

We left together, heading toward home. As we walked, Benjamin chatted away. "Uncle Geronimo, you were so nice to help that Ratbury truck driver. And you were so *brave* to save that old mouse," he squeaked. "When I grow up, I want to be just like you!"

I ruffled Benjamin's fur with my good paw. I loved that little mouse so much! I was proud that he wanted to be like me. I felt like a REAL HERO. No, I didn't have whiskers of steel. I didn't even have big mouscles. Still, I was so happy, I felt like I could carry ten mice on my shoulders.

Benjamin squeaked on about his school and his friends. Then, suddenly, he grew SERIOUS. He put his paw in his pocket and pulled out a wrapped present. "This is for you, Uncle. It's for Christmas," he said. "But you can open it now." I tore open the paper. Inside lay a small clay heart that was painted red. Scratched in the center were Benjamin's initials, **B.S.**

"It's a paperweight, Uncle Geronimo. For your desk," he explained. "That way my heart will always be close to you, even when we're apart!"

I was so touched. I had to wipe away a TEAR. Isn't my nephew the sweetest mouse on earth?

"My heart will always be close to you."

B.S.

COME SKATING
WITH ME . . .

On our way home, Benjamin and I stopped at the park. We made a **SNOWMOUSE**. It was so much fun!

We used a pinecone for the nose. We used some sticks for whiskers. Finally, we wrapped one of my

EXTRA-LONG RED SOCKS

around its neck for a scarf.

After that, we threw snowballs. Next, Benjamin talked me into renting a sled.

Last but not least, we skated on the *frozen pond*. We had a fabumouse time! Around and around we went, singing our favorite Christmas songs.

Come skating, come skating,

Come skating with me.
Come skating, come skating,
By the big fir tree.
Christmas Day is almost here,
Clap those paws and give a cheer!
Come skating, come skating,
Come skating with me!

MY NAME IS NIBBLETTE!

At last, we were ready to head home. Right then, I heard someone crying. It was a young female mouse about Benjamin's age. She was hiccuping with tears. A tough-looking young mouse stood over her. He was pulling one of her pigtails. He had tossed her backpack in the snow.

If there is one thing I can't stand, it's bully mice. "HEY, YOU!" I said sternly. "Leave her alone!"

The little thug marched over to me. Then he KICKED me in the shins.

I doubled over. Rats! That was painful! I slipped on the ice and fell, snout first, in the snow.

"Leave my uncle alone, you mean bully!" shouted Benjamin.

The other mouse RAN AWAY.

Benjamin picked up the backpack. He gave it to the young mouse.

"Don't worry about him," he told her. "He was just a COWARD. Did you see how he raced off?"

The little mouse wiped away her tears. "Thanks, that was very brave of you," she said shyly.

Benjamin turned bright **red**. I smiled. It looked like my little nephew had a new friend. Before

long, the two were holding paws and chattering away.

The little mouse told us her name was *Nibblette*. We all walked home together. On the way, we stopped at *The Slurpy Snout* for a **CUP** of hot **chocolate**. The *Snout* makes the best cocoa in New Mouse City.

We sat down at a corner table. Then

the waitress brought us our drinks.

I took a few sips. The steamy hot chocolate was topped with whipped cream. The cream stuck to my whiskers. I licked it off. I was wrong, I decided. The Snout didn't make the best cocoa in town. It made the best cocoa in the whole world! Yum!

A STRANGE SMELL
OF BURNING

It was already **DaRK**. We walked Nibblette home. Then we headed back to my mouse hole.

What a terrible Christmas Eve. First the Ratbury truck **ACCIDENT**, then the old mouse crossing the street, then that rotten bully kicking me in the shins. Things couldn't get any worse. I was glad I had everything set for the party. I couldn't do much decorating with one in a cast.

"I can't wait for your , Uncle Geronimo," Benjamin squeaked. "It's going to be so much fun!"

I smiled. Yes, it was going to be fun. I told Benjamin about my beautiful tree, my

CHRISTMAS GIFTS for the guests, and my refrigerator stocked with cheese.

I must say, I had outdone myself this year. It was going to be an absolutely perfect party.

We turned onto my block, MOUSEFORD LANE. At that moment, I was hit by a strange smell. What was it? It smelled like something burning. What a stench. It smelled worse than the time my uncle Hotpaw burned those ratburgers on his grill.

Suddenly, three fire trucks raced by. Their wailing sirens filled the night.

WHAT'S BURNING?

At the corner, I stopped a rodent walking by. "Pardon me, do you know **WHAT'S** on **FIRE?**" I asked.

The rodent nodded. "I heard that it's a **publisher's** home," he said.

I scratched my head. I didn't know there was another publisher living on Mouseford Lane. I thought I was the only one.

Before I could ask any more questions, the rodent continued. "Yes, it seems that the mouse left a Christmas candle burning," he added. "What a **cheesebrain!**"

Just then, an **AWFUL** thought hit me. I gulped.

Mouseford Lane? A publisher? A Christmas candle? **CHEESE NIBLETS!**

It was my very own home!

I elbowed my way through the crowd, followed by Benjamin.

"Make way! Make way! MY HOUSE is on fire!" I shrieked.

I finally reached 8 Mouseford Lane. But it was too late. My lovely home was going up in smoke!

What a dreadful Christmas Eve!

I'LL BET MY TAIL . . .

I wanted to scream. I wanted to **YELL**.
I wanted to twist my tail up in knots. But I
couldn't. My tail was still in bandages.

I sat down on the curb and sobbed. "My
Christmas tree . . . my wreath . . . my
gifts . . . my cheese pastries . . ." I muttered.
"What am I going to tell my guests?"

Benjamin tried to cheer me up. "It doesn't
matter, Uncle," he said. "We can all go to a
restaurant. And my present isn't important.
It's the thought that counts."

A firemouse aimed his hose into my
kitchen window. "I'll bet my tail you left a
CANDLE burning," he scolded. "This is
the tenth **fire** I'm putting out tonight. And
they all started with a burning candle."

I groaned. How could I have been so careless? *The Rodent's Gazette* always had stories about fires. Fires set by candle flames.

"You should thank your neighbor, Mrs. Meddlefur," the firemouse went on. "She called us right away."

I wasn't surprised. Mrs. Meddlefur was the nosiest neighbor around. She knew everybody's business. Now she ran up to me. "Mr. Stilton! I called as soon as I saw the **smoke**!" she cried. "But it was already too late."

I nodded, feeling sad. "Thanks anyway, Mrs. Meddlefur," I mumbled. What else could I say?

SOAKING WET PAWS

At last, the fire engines left. I stood in front of my beloved mouse hole. *Snout up, Geronimo,* I told myself. I opened my front door. Whoosh! I was hit by a flood of **wATEr**.

"Heeelp!" I cried as the current swept me away. Benjamin grabbed my tail before I ended up back on the street.

I went around checking out the damage. What a mess! The place was sopping wet. I stared at my precious belongings as they **floated by**.

I spotted a burned-up yellow object. It was

Benjamin's gift. In the kitchen, WATERY cheese slices stuck to the walls like glue. I felt like crying. All of my hard work. All of my decorating. It was all for nothing.

I stared glumly at my watery living room. I noticed that the window was wide open. The charred curtains twisted in the breeze. The ornament from my great-grandma Tanglefur lay on its side. Yes, that is what started the fire. A gust of wind must have blown the candle FLAME onto the curtains. I sighed. What is it that Sparky the Firemouse always teaches young rodents in school? **Never leave a burning flame unattended!** How could I have forgotten?

I sighed. I found two BUCKETS. I gave one to Benjamin. We began scooping up water. We tossed it outside.

The doorbell rang. I dragged myself to

the door. It was Thea and Trap.

"Big brother! What's happened?" my sister squeaked.

Trap stared closely at me, then at my home. "Gerrykins!" he cried. "Why did you start a **CAMPFIRE** in your home? And what's with the casts? You look like a furry M U M M Y ! "

I was so depressed. I HUNG MY HEAD. "First the truck, then the old mouse, then that rotten bully, then the candle . . ." I sobbed. "This is the worst Christmas Eve ever!"

I 🐾🐾🐾🐾🐾 into the kitchen. It was completely flooded. I cried and cried. I cried so hard, I began filling up the bucket with my own tears!

GET A GRIP, GERRY BERRY!

"Get a grip, Gerry Berry!" my sister exclaimed.

I stopped crying for a minute. Why do some mice like to make fun of my name? Is it really that hard to say? I don't think so. My sister just likes to drive me crazy. "The name is Geronimo!" I yelled now, stamping my paw. It splashed in a big puddle. Water shot up my nose.

Thea smirked. "Listen, Germeister!" she shouted at the top of her lungs. "Everything's under control! There will be a

Christmas Eve dinner here tonight, or my name is not Thea Stilton!" she shrieked. She jumped onto my TV stand and began barking out orders.

"Trap! Benjamin! This is what we need!" she began. Then she rattled off a long list of items.

— **one sump pump** (to suck up the water fast)

— **ten electric fans and ten heaters** (to dry the walls and floors)

— **new wallpaper** (to cover up the scorched walls)

— new wall-to-wall **carpeting** (to cover the floors ruined by the water)

— **a restorer** (to fix the priceless antique furniture)

— **lots of food** (to replace the spoiled Christmas Eve dinner)

When she was done with her list, Thea snapped her tail. "Well, what are you waiting for?!" she yelled. "Let's do it! Go! Go! Go!"

Did I mention my sister likes to be in charge?

Exhausted, I slumped into my favorite pawchair. "Forget it," I said with a sigh. "We'll never make it. It's impossible."

Oh, what a dreadful Christmas Eve!

NOTHING IS IMPOSSIBLE!

"Impossible?" Thea shrieked. "Nothing is impossible, Gerry dear!" she insisted. "You just have to try harder."

I rubbed my eyes. I was tired. So very tired. I was tired just thinking about trying. Forget the actual *doing*.

"But there's no time, Thea. The guests will be here in **one hour**. Just sixty **minutes**!" I whined.

Trap rolled his eyes. "Don't be such a crybaby, *Gerimonkey*," he scolded. "We can do it. We just have to work fast. And I've come up with the perfect plan for your *Christmas Eve* party. I've got lots of friends in New Mouse City. They'll help us get this shindig up and **squeaking!**

I let out a LOUD GROAN. I've met some of Trap's friends before. They're all a little wacky, if you ask me. His friend Slyrat liked to pretend he was a doctor to impress female mice. And his friend Splittail collected mousetraps for fun. Yes, I'd say they were all definitely wacky. Don't you agree?

Trap ignored my look of HORROR. He knew how I felt about his friends. Instead, he grabbed his cell phone. Soon, he was

happily chatting away. "I need a favor," I heard him squeak. "RIGHT NOW. . . . Yes, don't worry about the price. Money is no object. My cousin's paying for it," I heard him explain.

One thing you should know about my cousin. He loves spending money. Especially when it's not his own!

After a few more phone calls, he left. Benjamin followed him.

"Don't worry, Uncle, it's going to be all right!" my nephew whispered, giving me a kiss. I hoped he was right.

50'
FIFTY MINUTES TO PARTY TIME!

A little while later, a mouse came to the door. He had long sideburns. His PURPLE-AND-WHITE-striped sweater smelled like rotten fish.

"Well, look at this! You could sail a fishing boat in here!" he chuckled.

I didn't join him. My waterlogged mouse hole was nothing to laugh about. It was a tragedy. This smelly mouse had some nerve.

Just then, he stuck his paw out for me to shake. "The name's **Fishyfur**, but you can just call me **The Fish**," he said. "I'm Trap's friend. I'm the best fishermouse in town. These are my assistants. . . ."

Fishyfur aka *The Fish*

Two sailors popped up behind him. The Fish waved his paw at them. "OK, LET'S GET GOING, ratoids!" he ordered. "We've got work to do!"

The two sailor mice brought out a long **rubber tube**. They connected it to a generator. One mouse put the generator on his back like a backpack. Then they began pumping up water by the gallon. The water shot out of the window.

I heard a big **SPLASH** down below. Angry voices followed.

"What's going on?"

"Where's all this water coming from?"

"It's a **FLASH FLOOD!**"

"Look, it's coming from Stilton's apartment!"

"Stilton?"

"Yes, Stilton, the publisher! If I get my paws on him . . ."

I gulped. The two sailors sniggered.

Right then, The Fish caught sight of Thea. His jaw dropped. Birds sang. Heart bubbles floated over his head. Well, maybe there were no birds or bubbles. But I could tell it was *love* at first sight. My sister has that effect on male mice.

The Fish bowed before her. "Princess of Perfection! *Goddess of Gorgeousness!* I never knew Trap had such a stunning cousin," he murmured. "Are you free tonight, Queen of **Queens**? How about a nice seafood *dinner* with The Fish?" he said, curling his whiskers. "I know the most wonderfully **romantic** place. . . ."

Thea fluttered her eyelashes. "Take care of this water first," she squeaked. "Then we'll see about dinner."

I was fuming. What was Thea thinking?

She couldn't have dinner with this SMELLY MOUSE. It was *Christmas Eve*. She would be having dinner at my house! "Can you cut the chatter!" I yelled. "I am expecting lots of guests in less than one hour! Please, hurry up!"

The Fish snorted. "Wow. Someone has his cranky coat on today," he jeered.

I chewed my whiskers. This mouse was driving me batty. But I needed him. So I closed my eyes and counted to ten. When I opened them, a miracle had occurred. The floor was completely dry.

"Thank you! Thank you! Thank you!" I squeaked. "How much do I owe you?"

The Fish just winked at my sister. "It's on me," he said. "A *gift* for your beautiful sister."

40'
FORTY MINUTES TO PARTY TIME!

After The Fish left, a **plump** mouse came to the door. He was dressed in a purple velvet suit. Yes, you heard me. A PURPLE velvet suit! Around his neck he wore a **CHAIN** with a big ugly charm. On his feet, he wore green snakeskin shoes. *What an outfit,* I thought. *What a perfectly horrible, hideous outfit! Didn't this mouse have any friends?* I wondered. How could they let him scamper out of his mouse hole dressed like that?

Before I could ask, he stuck out his paw. "Hello, there, I'm Trap's friend," he began. *Well, that explained the outfit,* I thought.

"I'm Cheddar E. Gadget. I'm an appliance salesmouse. I'm here to dry your place out."

In one paw, he held up one **tiny** fan. In the other, he had one **tiny** heater.

I groaned. "One fan! One heater? That's not enough!" I squeaked.

Cheddar gave me the once-over. Then he shook his head.

"You must be Geronimeister," he smirked. "Trap told me you have terrible taste in clothes."

My mouth dropped open. Steam poured from my ears. He had to be joking. I could be on the cover of *G.Q. Mouse* magazine compared to this clown!

Cheddar E. Gadget

But I ignored his insult and held my tongue.

Cheddar patted the **tiny** fan with his paw. "I'll have you know that this is a one-of-a-kind turbo fan," he boasted. "And this is the *super-duper-micro-macro-mouse* heater 500," he went on. Then he looked me in the eye. "In fact, I'll bet you a **ton of cheese** that I can dry your whole place in ten minutes!"

I snorted. Did this mouse think I was born yesterday?

Before I could squeak, he switched on the **HEATER**. Seconds later, it was as hot as the Rattytrap Jungle in the summertime. Then he switched on the fan. Suddenly, it was like

being in the Mousehara desert. The only things missing were the sand and the camels!

I was having trouble breathing. It was so hot and dry, I began to feel FAINT. I had to get out. I stumbled down the stairs. Then I plopped down on the curb outside of my building. Ah, FRESH AIR.

Ten minutes later, some mouse was calling me. I looked up. Cheddar was hanging outside my window. "You can come on in now!" he called. "I told you I work fast."

Back in my house, I touched the walls. Cheesecake! They were completely dry! I couldn't believe it!

I turned to Cheddar. "Amazing!" I gasped. "What do I owe you?"

Cheddar just grinned. "Don't worry about it, Gerry Berry," he said. "I owe Trap a favor. But maybe you'd like to buy my turbo fan and heater."

I didn't really want Cheddar's appliances. I mean, I wasn't expecting any more floods. Still, I guess anything could happen. What if a hurricane hit? What if an **earthquake** knocked my house into the ocean? What if a big hairy cat monster spit gobs of drool down my chimney? Hey, you never know. I decided I shouldn't take any chances.

With a sigh, I grabbed my **CHECKBOOK**.

THIRTY MINUTES TO PARTY TIME!

A few minutes later, there was another knock on my door. I opened it.

Eight workmice stared back at me. One had a ladder. A couple had toolboxes. Another had rolls of wallpaper.

"We're **THE PAWS BROTHERS!**" they all shouted as one.

"You name it, we can fix it! Yesirree,

THE PAWS BROTHERS

you're in good paws with the Paws!" shrieked the fattest one, whose name was Plumpy. He let out a high-pitched squeak of laughter.

I jumped. Then I smiled politely. "You must be Trap's friends," I said.

Plumpy shook his head. It seems the Paws Brothers had never met my cousin until that day. "He came into our shop, The Repair Rat," Plumpy explained. "He said you were desperate. You needed NEW WALLPAPER and new CARPETING. He said it was an emergency job. A big emergency. He said you would pay us a ton of money."

I shook my head. Trap was right. This was an emergency job. But did he have to say I would PAW over big bucks? I wasn't made of money. I was going broke by the hour! I was going to have to break into my mousey bank if this kept up!

Still, what could I do? My guests would arrive in less than thirty minutes. Yes, I was DESPERATE. I gave the Paws Brothers the go-ahead. They got to work right away. Ten minutes later, they were done. That's right, I said ten minutes! And I mean completely done! My house had NEW PAPER ON THE WALLS. And the floors were covered with brand-new wall-to-wall carpeting. It was amazing. It was astounding. It was the most expensive carpeting on the planet!

sob...

20'

TWENTY MINUTES TO PARTY TIME!

As soon as the Paws Brothers left, a dignified-looking rodent appeared at the door.

"Good evening, I am *Professor Parker Preciousfur*," he said. "I am an expert in antiques. Your cousin Trap said you needed some restoring done."

I shook his paw. "Thank you for coming, Professor," I squeaked. "I hope you can save my cherished antique furniture. It's so important to me." It was true. I love antiques. I had furnished my whole home with them. Yes, I know they were expensive. But to me they were worth it. Old chairs made during the Great Cat War. Old tables from the

Early Muenster Period. It was like owning pieces of history.

The professor pulled out a tiny magnifying glass. He put it up to his eye. Then he examined the furniture. After a while, he wrinkled his snout. "May I ask you where you bought this furniture?" he said.

I turned pale. "Of course. I bought it all from *Woodrat's Relics*," I said.

Now the professor had a horrified expression on his face. He reached over and patted my paw. "I am so sorry," he said. "*Woodrat* is the biggest swindler in town. These are not real antiques. They are just reproductions."

I felt **FAINT**. I felt sick. I felt like the dumbest mouse on the block.

Professor Parker Preciousfur

The professor told me not to worry. He said he could still help. He would remove the old furniture and replace it with new stuff. Well, not really new stuff, I mean old stuff. I mean not old stuff, but *antique stuff*. You get the idea. Anyway, it turned out the professor owned a store just next to *Woodrat's*. It was called Professor Preciousfur's Priceless Antiques.

He whipped out a catalog. "Take a look at this gorgeous mahogany bookcase," he murmured. "And here's a beautiful turn-of-the-century dining room table. It seats up to twenty rodents!"

I stumbled off to get my checkbook. "**I'll take everything**," I said with a sigh. What else could I do? I couldn't expect my guests to sit on the floor.

Ten minutes later, the furniture was in place.

TEN MINUTES TO PARTY TIME!

Before I could try out one of my new chairs, the doorbell rang. I opened it. Thirty rodents marched inside. They wore white waiter **uniforms**. They were carrying platters of food. Behind them strode a **PLUMP** mouse. He had *curled* whiskers and a sly smile. I recognized him right away. It was the famous chef **Saucy Le Paws**. He had his own television show, *Slice and Dice for Mice!* I was so surprised to see him. But I was even more surprised to see who was with him.

It was none other than my cousin Trap!

My cousin waved his paw in the air. "Bet you didn't know I was Saucy's friend, did you, Gerrykins?" he smirked. "We went to *Little Tails Academy* together. He made the best spitballs in class!"

My jaw hit the ground. Saucy Le Paws? The famous chef? Made spitballs? I thought he only made gourmet cheese balls!

Before I could ask, Trap thumped me on the back. "Tonight is your lucky night, Geronimoid," he squeaked. "Saucy has agreed to cook for you!"

Saucy Le Paws

X
PARTY TIME AT LAST!

Soon, the dining room table was filled with food. A beautiful cheese tower stood as a **centerpiece**. Each place was set with my *best china*. Yes, it had survived the fire! Unfortunately, my tablecloth wasn't as lucky. It was burned to a crisp. But Thea came up with a great idea. She pulled down my red velvet curtains. Then she draped them over the **IMMENSE** table.

I must admit, everything looked incredible. I was shocked. I mean, I'm not much of a last-minute mouse. I like to plan. And plan. And plan some more. Thea says I need to relax. She says I should learn to go with the flow. Maybe I will try. I just need to know when the flow is coming. How long it will stay. And if it's going to eat dinner.

It was nine o'clock sharp. Party time.

The **doorbell** rang. Hmm . . . whatever happened to fashionably late? Oh, well. It didn't matter. I was ready for my first guest. I swung open the door. But it wasn't a guest. It was a delivery mouse from Better Cheddar and Beyond. He had the two CHEESE BASKETS I had bought this morning. Was it only this morning? It seemed like a million years ago. I stared at the baskets. They would make perfect presents for Thea and Trap.

A couple of minutes later, the doorbell rang again. Was this one of my guests? No. It was a delivery mouse from the toy shop. He gave me the STUFFED cat I had bought.

"Merry Christmas, my dear nephew," I

said, presenting it to Benjamin.

He hugged it tight. "Thank you, Uncle," he whispered. "You are the best."

The doorbell rang once more. Was it another delivery? No. This time it really was the first guest. "Geronimo, my darling nephew," squeaked my aunt Sweetfur. Aunt Sweetfur is my favorite aunt. She lives a few blocks away. She is always forgetting things like her glasses and her house keys. Once she even forgot her own birthday. But she never forgets me. Now she handed me a gift. It was a beautiful hand-knit scarf. "Oh, thank you, Auntie," I gushed, giving her a hug.

The bell was ringing again.

Aunt Sweetfur

Cousin Stevie Stingysnout

Samuel S. Stingysnout

It was my **uncle Samuel S. Stingysnout**. Uncle Samuel was one cheap mouse. He never gave anyone anything. Not even the time. Now he shook my paw. "I brought you something, too, Geronimo," he smirked. I gasped.

AUNT SUGARFUR

UNCLE KINDPAWS

Uncle Walter Worrywhiskers

twin daughters Squeakette and Squeakella

Could Uncle Stingysnout have changed his cheapskate ways? Then he stepped aside. "Say hello to my son, Stevie Stingysnout. HA-HA-HA!" Uncle Samuel roared.

I laughed politely at his joke. I'm surprised he didn't charge me for it.

Uncle Samuel was followed by my AUNT SUGARFUR and UNCLE KINDPAWS and their twin daughters, Squeakette and Squeakella. The two young mice pawed me a huge package. "This is for you, Uncle Geronimo!" they squeaked shyly.

I opened it. It was a tin of chocolate-covered Cheesy Chews. Yum! My favorite!

Behind them stood Uncle Walter Worrywhiskers. Uncle Wally is a champion **WORRYWART**. He is especially worried about germs. He didn't shake my paw. Too many germs, I guess. "You haven't invited anyone with a cold, have you?" he asked. Then he gave me a gift. It was a box of herbal cough drops.

I was startled by a loud whistle. It was my UNCLE GAGRAT, always the prankster. He pawed me a small box. I opened it carefully. A boxing glove sprang out and PUNCHED me in the snout.

"Slimy Swiss rolls!" I cried.

Uncle Gagrat smacked his side. "Ha-ha! Tricked you again, Nephew," he snorted.

"You got me, all right," I murmured politely.

Slimy Swiss rolls!

UNCLE GAGRAT

Uncle Mastermouse

The doorbell rang again. It was my uncle Mastermouse. He was a top professor at NEW MOUSE CITY UNIVERSITY. He pawed me a thick book. I read the title, *War and Cheese*. It was so heavy, I almost dropped it.

Right behind him came my grandfather **William Shortpaws**. Grandfather was the founder of *The Rodent's Gazette*. He had given me the newspaper. And he never let me forget it. Yes, it was like a gift that kept on giving. Kept on giving me a headache, that is!

"How's the company

William Shortpaws

TINA SPICYTAIL

doing, Nephew?" he barked. "I hope you are following my rules. I started that paper, you know. And I can take it back!"

I gave him a weak smile. I had heard this song and dance before.

Next to Grandfather was his faithful *housekeeper*, Tina Spicytail. Tina was famous for her **triple-cheese lasagna**. She was a tough old mouse. I guess that's why she and Grandfather got along so well.

Dr. Edward S. Smugrat III

Silky Fur

Before long, my living room was filled with rodents of every size, shape, and color.

Besides my close family, I had also invited friends. I looked around. There was Dr. Edward S. Smugrat III. He was a snobbish rat I had met at The Ratking Golf Club. And there was Silky Fur, a pretty lady friend. I played tennis with her on Thursdays.

Of course, all of my friends at *The Rodent's Gazette* were invited, too. My secretary, Mousella MacMouser. My editor in chief, Sweetie Cheesetriangle. And yes, a party wouldn't be a party without **Pinky Pick**, my assistant editor.

Thea's friends had come, too. They were everywhere. That mouse has more friends than Cheeseball the Clown at the circus! I glanced around. I spotted *Swissita Tenderfur*, **FREDDY FASTPAWS**, and a smooth-talking mouse who called himself **Sniff**. Yes, Thea's friends were all over. Squeaking, eating, laughing . . .

Still, no one was laughing as loud as one

FREDDY FASTPAWS

group of rodents. They were Trap's friends. What an odd bunch. One rodent was dressed as a giant slice of Swiss cheese. Did he think it was Halloween? Another did not speak. He YELLED EVERYTHING. My ears rang when I stood near him. Then there was the rat who never stopped whistling. I finally stuck a cheese stick in his mouth. I know it is rude. But he was giving me a mouse-sized headache!

My nephew Benjamin had invited his new friend, *Nibblette*. I watched the two of them holding paws and giggling. They were so cute.

Benjamin and Nibblette

At last, the doorbell stopped ringing. I ran over to my stereo. Did it survive the fire?

I turned on some cheery holiday music. Cheesecake! The Christmas jingle filled the room.

Cheddar balls, cheddar balls,
Cheddar all the way.
Oh, what fun it is to eat sharp cheese
on Christmas Day-ay!

Just then, Saucy Le Paws marched out of the kitchen. He twirled his long whiskers. Then he cleared his throat.

"Ladies and gentlemice!"

he bellowed.

"Dinner is served!"

MERRY CHRISTMAS TO YOU, TOO!

We sat down to a delicious feast. I was enjoying a plate of steaming nachos when I heard Pinky whispering to Mousella.

"I wonder what Sally Ratmousen is doing tonight," she giggled. "What a rotten rat!"

Do you know Sally Ratmousen? She runs *The Daily Rat.* She is my number one enemy.

"I heard she's spending Christmas Eve alone," Mousella answered, shaking her head.

"Serves her right," Trap added. "That rodent is as mean as a rabid tiger cat!"

Right then, Saucy set out

another tray of food. I looked around at the happy snouts of *all* my guests. Everyone was laughing and squeaking. It was such a warm and friendly sight.

Suddenly, I was overcome with *sadness*. *Poor Sally Ratmousen,* I thought. Yes, she was my enemy. Yes, she was rude. Yes, she was obnoxious. Yes, she was an all-around pain-in-my-fur. But it was Christmas Eve. No mouse should be alone on such a *special* night.

Before I could stop myself, I picked up the phone and dialed Sally's number. "Hello? Is this Sally Ratmousen? This is *Geronimo Stilton*," I squeaked.

For a moment, there was total silence. Then Sally's **gruff** voice came over the line. "What do you want, Stilton?" she asked warily.

I explained I was having a *Christmas Eve* dinner party. Then I asked her to join us.

Another long silence followed. I think Sally was in shock. As I said, we are rivals. We don't call each other to talk. We just call each other names.

"It's *Christmas Eve*, Sally," I added. "Let's call a truce."

After a while, Sally agreed. "All right," she SNORTED. "But just this once. And only because it's *Christmas*."

I chuckled. Sally would never change!

Three minutes later, she was at my front door. She pawed me a **tiny box**.

"This is for you," she grunted.

I opened it. It was a tiny *silver frame* with Sally's picture in it. *"To my friend-*

foe," Sally had written on the back. "Merry Christmas while the truce lasts."

I grinned. Then I invited her in.

"Thanks, Sally," I said. "And Merry Christmas! Merry Christmas to you, too!"

ABOUT THE AUTHOR

Born in New Mouse City, Mouse Island, Geronimo Stilton is Rattus Emeritus of Mousomorphic Literature and of Neo-Ratonic Comparative Philosophy. For the past twenty years, he has been running *The Rodent's Gazette*, New Mouse City's most widely read daily newspaper.

Stilton was awarded the Ratitzer Prize for his scoop on *The Curse of the Cheese Pyramid*. He has also received the Andersen 2000 Prize for Personality of the Year. One of his best-sellers won the 2002 eBook Award for world's best ratlings' electronic book. His works have been published all over the globe.

In his spare time, Mr. Stilton collects antique cheese rinds and plays golf. But what he most enjoys is telling stories to his nephew Benjamin.

Don't miss any of my other fabumouse adventures!

Be sure to check out these very special editions!

THE KINGDOM OF FANTASY

THE QUEST FOR PARADISE:
THE RETURN TO THE KINGDOM OF FANTASY

And look for this new series about my friend Creepella von Cacklefur!

#1 THE THIRTEEN GHOSTS

#2 MEET ME IN HORRORWOOD

If you like my brother's books, you'll love mine!

**THEA STILTON
AND THE
DRAGON'S CODE**

**THEA STILTON
AND THE
MOUNTAIN OF FIRE**

**THEA STILTON
AND THE GHOST OF
THE SHIPWRECK**

**THEA STILTON
AND THE
SECRET CITY**

**THEA STILTON
AND THE MYSTERY
IN PARIS**

**THEA STILTON
AND THE CHERRY
BLOSSOM ADVENTURE**

**THEA STILTON
AND THE
STAR CASTAWAYS**

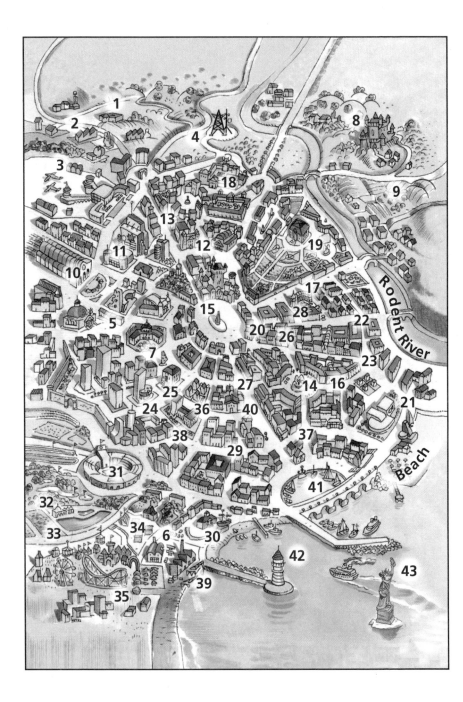

Map of New Mouse City

1. Industrial Zone
2. Cheese Factories
3. Angorat International Airport
4. WRAT Radio and Television Station
5. Cheese Market
6. Fish Market
7. Town Hall
8. Snotnose Castle
9. The Seven Hills of Mouse Island
10. Mouse Central Station
11. Trade Center
12. Movie Theater
13. Gym
14. Catnegie Hall
15. Singing Stone Plaza
16. The Gouda Theater
17. Grand Hotel
18. Mouse General Hospital
19. Botanical Gardens
20. Cheap Junk for Less (Trap's store)
21. Parking Lot
22. Museum of Modern Art
23. University and Library
24. *The Daily Rat*
25. *The Rodent's Gazette*
26. Trap's House
27. Fashion District
28. The Mouse House Restaurant
29. Environmental Protection Center
30. Harbor Office
31. Mousidon Square Garden
32. Golf Course
33. Swimming Pool
34. Blushing Meadow Tennis Courts
35. Curlyfur Island Amusement Park
36. Geronimo's House
37. New Mouse City Historic District
38. Public Library
39. Shipyard
40. Thea's House
41. New Mouse Harbor
42. Luna Lighthouse
43. The Statue of Liberty

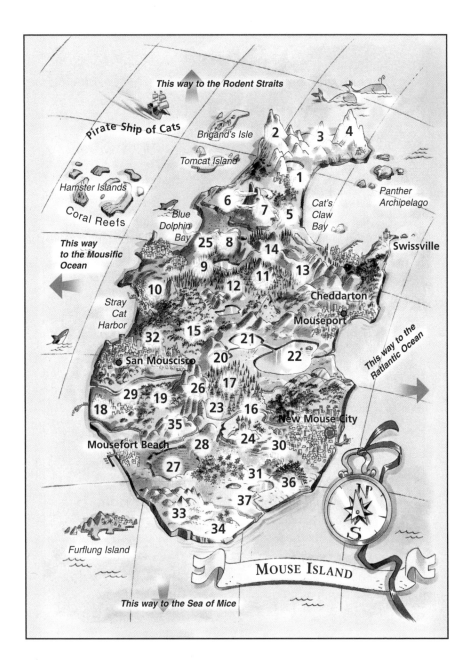

Map of Mouse Island

1. Big Ice Lake
2. Frozen Fur Peak
3. Slipperyslopes Glacier
4. Coldcreeps Peak
5. Ratzikistan
6. Transratania
7. Mount Vamp
8. Roastedrat Volcano
9. Brimstone Lake
10. Poopedcat Pass
11. Stinko Peak
12. Dark Forest
13. Vain Vampires Valley
14. Goose Bumps Gorge
15. The Shadow Line Pass
16. Penny Pincher Lodge
17. Nature Reserve Park
18. Las Ratayas Marinas
19. Fossil Forest
20. Lake Lake
21. Lake Lake Lake
22. Lake Lakelakelake
23. Cheddar Crag
24. Cannycat Castle
25. Valley of the Giant Sequoia
26. Cheddar Springs
27. Sulfurous Swamp
28. Old Reliable Geyser
29. Vole Vail
30. Ravingrat Ravine
31. Gnat Marshes
32. Munster Highlands
33. Mousehara Desert
34. Oasis of the Sweaty Camel
35. Cabbagehead Hill
36. Rattytrap Jungle
37. Rio Mosquito

Dear mouse friends,
Thanks for reading, and farewell
till the next book.
It'll be another whisker-licking-good
adventure, and that's a promise!

Geronimo Stilton